This book belongs to

....

....

'for Hazel, with love' Jill Newton

This edition published in 2016 by Alligator Publishing Ltd.
Cupcake is an imprint of Alligator Publishing Ltd.
2nd Floor, 314 Regents Park Road, London N3 2JX

Written and illustrated by Jill Newton

Printed in China 0353

Titch the Tiddler

cupcake

Titch watched the big, bold fish laugh and play by the old shipwreck. He swam towards them to join in.

"What are you doing here?" laughed Puffa. "This is not the place for small fry!"

All the big fish roared with laughter at poor little Titch the Tiddler.

"Hee, hee!"

Titch so wanted to be like them.

He'd love to be able to make a big splash like **Whale**.

SPLASH!

To be able to blow himself up and be **big** and spiky like **Puffa**.

Now that would be great . . .

Or have razor-sharp, shiny teeth like

Shark.

Even to be able to dance as gracefully as the sea horses did would be lovely.

But his splash was more like a little plop.

PLOP!

He didn't have a **single** tooth to his name.

Blowing himself up simply
made his scales hurt.

And as for dancing.

Well, it was as far away from
being graceful as you could
possibly imagine.

"I'd say you're perfect as you are, even if the big fish don't want to play with you," said his mum.

"And the crabs and octopuses love you. You're always finding little hidden treasures for them in the shipwreck. And the baby fish – they have great fun playing hide and seek with you."

But somehow that wasn't enough for Titch.

He wanted to be **big** and **bold** like the others.

So Titch got some pointy shells and stuck them to his back.

He tied a large scallop shell to his tail to help him swim fast.

He wrapped slippy, slimy seaweed around his fins.

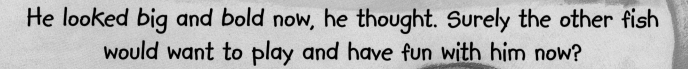

He looked big and bold now, he thought. Surely the other fish would want to play and have fun with him now?

The big, bold fish did have fun. But not the kind that Titch wanted to be part of.

"Look at the Tiddler!" shrieked Shark.

"He's trying to be fierce!"

"Hee, hee!"

The big, bold fish were laughing so much they did not notice that the sunlight had disappeared. And the sea had gone dark . . .

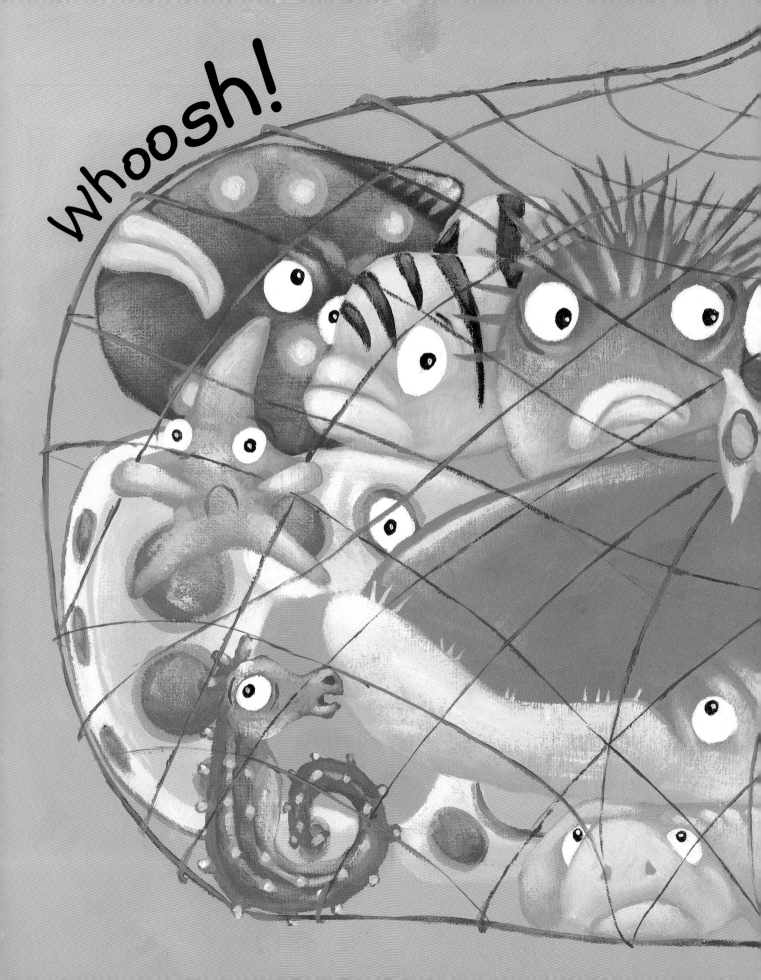

A large net was pulled tight around the fish who were not laughing any more. They were trapped. No one could escape.

No one except . . .

Titch.

Titch swam through the holes in the net.

"Please help us!" the prisoners yelled.

So little Titch the Tiddler swam away as fast as his little fins could carry him, back towards the shipwreck.

The **big**, bold fish did not feel **big** or bold as the net slowly heaved them upwards.

They felt afraid and very alone.

But not for long!

Shark, Whale, Turtle and all their trapped gang could not believe their eyes when they saw an army of octopuses and a cavalry of crabs dashing their way.

And leading this army was a tiny yellow fish. A tiddler of a fish.

Titch the Tiddler!

He had brought his friends to help.

The army of helpers quickly set about the net.

SNIP!

SNIP!

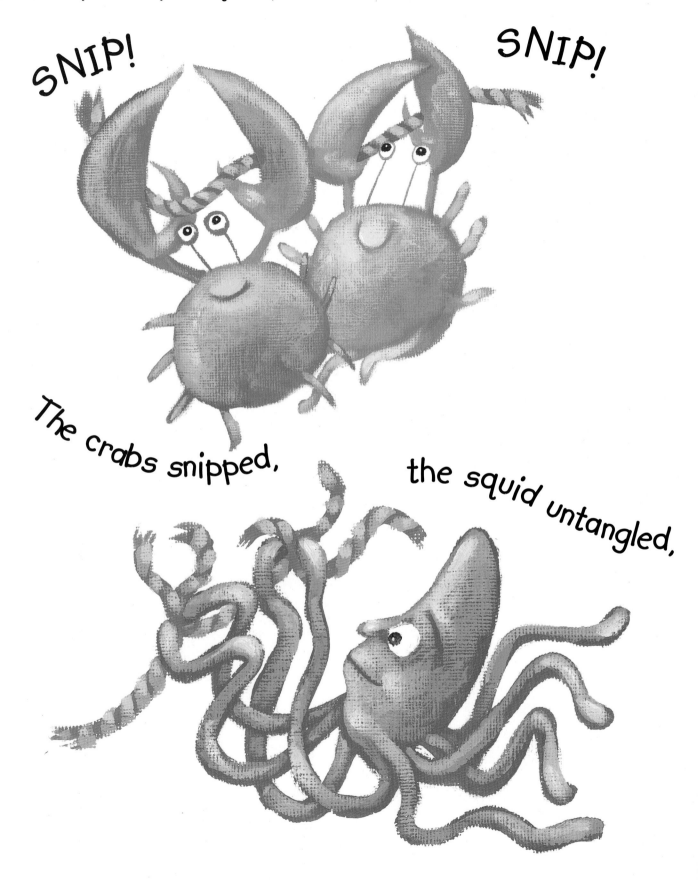

The crabs snipped,

the squid untangled,

the octopuses unravelled

and Titch tugged and pulled,

pulled and tugged,

with all his might until . . .

. . . the fish
were free!

They rushed over to Titch and his
helpers who were resting on the rocks.

Rescuing was quite hard work.

"Thank you,
oh thank you so much!"
they cried.

"Can we ask just **one** more thing, Mr Titch Tiddler, hero of the sea?" asked Shark.

"You can ask," said the little tired fish warily.

"Can we play here with you? It does look like **fun**."

Titch thought for a while. "On one condition," he replied.

"**Anything**," nodded Shark. "That we play **hide and seek!**" yelled Titch, zooming off to hide. They all had hours and hours of fun searching for him.

Can **YOU** find him?

The End.